THIS BOOK BELONGS TO:

THE YARN NAMED SUN

"Hello, Yarn! Good morning to you!"

The little ball of yarn said to itself as it stretched. It poked its loose end out through the gap at the top of the drawer of the bedside table where the light in. Soon it had managed to slideall the way through andjumped out and rolled around the room.

"Wooooow! It's an obstacle course!"

It slipped under the bed, a couple of chairs, and right under the wardrobe.

"Hey Yarn!" Tosha said, Stop fooling around I want to do some knitting today!"

She took the yarn from under the wardrobe and put it on the windowsill. Thenshe picked up the knitting needles from the shelf, took the end of the yarn, and sat down by the window.

"Well, will it be ready soon?" said the yarn, wanting everything to happen faster. It got so excited that it began swaying from side to side and suddenly fell from the windowsill onto the floor.

"Is it ready yet?!" It asked every minute.

Like all little yarns, it was a bit of a fidget, always wanting to jump and play. It really wanted to explore the world and find out about itself.

"I wonder who I will become in this life?" The ball asked itself.

"I've been friends with Purr the cat for a long time, and she has her own name. She is called Purr because her purring calms and balances everything. She knows how to warm and comfort. What is my name?"

The yarn knew very little about life. In fact he knew practically nothing. All he knew was the small bright room of his mistress Tosha – no different from that dark drawer, only larger.

"If only I could become like Purr," it dreamed. "She can go where she wants, travel to different places. That's so exciting!" It and the cat often played together, tumbling in the warm bright sunny spot on the baggy sofa, meeting the summer morning sun streaming through the open window. Purr would roll about the yarn with the soft pads of her paws, trying to grab it, but the yarn was very nimble and always tangled her in its woollen arms, saying: "That's it for you!!" The yarn was very curious and asked a lot of questions. It was interested in every little thing. Once Purr said that it looked like the sun, just as warm and just as round!

"Purr, purr – I'm rolling my own little sun," she purred in pleasure.

"Maybe I am a little sun? But the sun lives in the sky, and it's so high up!" The yarn thought to itself.

"Maybe the sun lives somewhere else as well as the sky?"

"Purr, purr – in the sea, in the waterrrr," Purr replied. "Every evening I see the sun rolling down and going into the sea, into the waterrrr!"

And the yarn, together with Purr, came up with a smart plan. They decided to run away the moment Tosha sat down again to knit. The two agreed that today was today was the day of their BIG ADVENTURE – the bold and rolling yarn and its nimble furry sidekick!

After breakfast, Tosha sat down happily to knit, and Purr purred at her feet. The cuckoo clock on the wall swung its pendulum. The hands approached nine o'clock. The curtains on the windows and doors swayed in the sea breeze. Then suddenly Purr jumped on the yarn, pushed it with her paws, and began to roll it to the front door.

"Purr, what are you up to now! Oh, you little rascal!" Tosha cried out crossly.

"I just brought the needles together!"

But Purr wasn't listening, and the yarn was too happy to just stop. It quickly rolled down the steps of the porch and out of the gate. Ahead was a world full of amazing adventures.

"Hey! Hold on! Stop! – Where are you off to?" shouted Tosha, grabbing the knitting needles and the work that she had just started tightly.

But the yarn rolled out and away along the seashore. Wow! It had never felt the sand before! How warm it was! How it slipped and slid so softly. The yarn dug into the sand, and the sand tickled it, sneaking under it threads. Oh, what fun!

"And the sea? What wonderful sounds! How the waves roar! I heard it before through the window, but I had no idea that it was so wide!"

He rolled to the sea's edge and peered over the water, as it reflected the cloudy sky, and thought:

"I will make friends with you!"

The yarn stretched out a part of its string to touch the wave but could suddenly hardly lift it from the ground.

"Help! Help! The water's made it so heavy! I'm going under"

It was quickly unwinding and being tugged into the sea! But just in time, the little yarn found itself being wound in skilfully by familiar hands, hands that knew how to roll it back together again.

"Well now – I got you!" Tosha said with a satisfied look. "Now you can't run away!"

Suddenly, they heard a terrible hissing under their feet. Tosha looked down and saw she was standing on what looked like a strange branch sticking out of a bush. But the branch lunged at her and hurled her back violently. Then the sand bulged up and quivered like the mouth of a volcano! Moments later a huge mouth with sharp teeth erupted from the sand, and started snapping moved towards her. Purr bristled, protecting her mistress. Yarn knew just what to do. It leaped boldly from Tosha's hand and sped towards the monster. After a terrible flurry and kerfuffle, the monster began to realize that he was getting hopelessly tangled in wool and losing strength. The more the monster struggled the more it got tangled and tired. Finally, the monster gave up and yarn wrapped it round entirely from head to toe. The monster stood motionless a couple of steps away from Tosha. It gurgled and tried to snap its teeth. Tosha was very scared. It was a crocodile!

"What a monster! It could swallow me whole in an instant!"

But gradually, she realized that the crocodile was entirely tied up!

"Oh, brilliant job, my yarn, oh, brilliant job, you little daredevil!" Tosha sang out joyfully.

The yarn turned crimson from such praise, but not so you'd see.

Oh, oh, oh the monstrous crocodile

Got trapped in a net, and lost its smile.

The toothy beast's in a right old tangle,

Can't wriggle its way out from any angle.

What a tricky spot! Tied in knots!

"Yikes!" said the croc, "I feel such a clot!

They say I'm fierce and snappy, but look at me fool –

Tamed in a trice by a little ball of wool!"

"I'm a crocodile tamer!" said the little yarn.

"Well, monster, will you still roar and bite?" said Tosha

Now the croc was looking worried. He thought: "Will I really be tied up like this my forever? Oh, if only I could get free, I would never eat anyone again." The yarn realized what the crocodile wanted to say, but the thread was bunched into an absolute mess of knots – impossible to do without the help of a person. Tosha decided to help the crocodile. The thread was everywhere, on its claws, its spines and even its teeth. It wasn;t easy to unravel the terrible creature, but Tosha had golden hands and a brave heart.

"Shhhhh!" The crocodile hissed, asking for forgiveness from its liberator, and crawling into the nearest puddle. But it was still a fierce crocodile.

So Tosha, holding the yarn, gathered pebbles and laid them around the puddle, speaking soothingly as she turned the puddle into a magnificent pool. A smart bathing for crocodiles! When Tosha and the yarn left, saying goodbye, the crocodile splashed and tumbled for a long time, saying:

"What a pool! No crocodile in the world has such a pool! I am the happiest crocodile in the world, because everyone has a sea, rivers, but no other croc has their own pool."

Tosha and the yarn headed home. But they they went right past the house to the main road. The yarn sat in the pocket of his mistress's dress, like a baby kangaroo in its mother's pouch.

"We'll go along this road, and then turn to the 'Quiet Harbour," Tosha said to the ball. Quiet Harbour was the name of the nearby village by the sea.

"It's better to go through the village. There are no wild crocodiles there. This is a safe path, but the road ahead is long," she added.

"Long road?!" Thought the ball. "I wonder how long it is? It can't possibly be longer than me!"

And he decided to check how long the road was and jumped out of Tosha's pocket.

"Jump-jump-jump, jump-jump-jump,

I am yarn - a cuddly clump."

He was humming a song when suddenly...

"Stop! Where are you rushing off to?" Shouted a man on a motorcycle.

"Careful!" A blue van hummed.

The yarn turned quickly, and rolled right across a pedestrian crossing.

He did not know the rules of the road, which say that you should not rush across crossings. A car with a man and a dog inside and loaded luggage was speeding towards him. The man noticed the little yarn too late and ran right over it. By the time the car slowed down, the yarn was already at the rear wheel.

"Hey!" Tosha screamed.

The yarn was flat as pancake.

The bags and suitcases on the roof of the car shot forward and fell all over the road.

"Beep-beep-beep!" Hooted the other cars!

"Dooooooo!" The big truck was angry.

Tosha quickly ran up to the baby yarn and carried him out of the way.

After this, drivers began to scold the yarn, saying:

"Yarns have no place on the road, yarns need to stay in the arts and crafts club!"

And then the yarn welled up. First came a single tear then a second, and soon his tears began to flow like a stream. Soon the wool was swelling up with all the moisture. He thought that he would stay flat and fat for the rest of his life, and sobbed:

"I'll never be a yarn again! I will be ugly and useless forever!"

But for Tosha he would always be a beautiful yarn, because she loves him very much. After some time, she made the yarn shaped like a large pancake, into a shape like a ball – more like a yarn should. The yarn immediately cheered up.

"Wow! I can be different! I can be small and big, flat and round! Incredible!"

Soon the traffic wardens arrived to give them a penalty.

One wrote something down in a notebook and scolded Tosha:

"You can't play on the roads with yarns! It's very dangerous!"

The yarn realized that because of him Tosha got scolded. He promised himself that he never again be naughty on the roads.

Tosha moved on with the yarn and Purr. They turned into the Quiet Harbour and walked through the outskirts of the village. Soon they came to the coast. By then, the yarn was dry and more like its normal size.

"We need a rest," Tosha said and sat down on the sand. Waves rolled onto the shore, foaming and splashing. Tosha and Purr dozed off.

As she woke up Tosha felt a poweful breath on her leg and froze with terror. She kept her eyes shut, but she felt something big and wet and rough touching her right knee. She squinted one eye open and there she saw a huge tiger staring straight at her. It was growling quietly. The yarn, lying nearby on the sand, woke up too and thought: "Any second now he will attack my mistress!" So it suddenly jumped right on the tiger's nose. The tiger was stunned, his paw involuntarily reached for the yarn. Then a completely strange picture appeared before Tosha's eyes. The tiger began to play with the yarn, like a small kitten.

"Incredible!" thought Tosha.

Oh my my! Cheeky little yarn ball –

Playing with a tiger, not scared at all!

Just a soft and bouncy ball of woolly fluff

Who would believe that it could be so tough?

But is the fierce tiger up for such games?

He's a wild, wild beast and not very tame!

He's teeth sharp as knives, mighty claws and that,

Yes he's a scary, scary tiger, not a tabby cat!

But the tiger tumbled, jumped, lay on its back, tossed the ball up, juggling it like a circus performer! It was a real circus show! And the yarn was just happy to play. After all, it was it always did with Purr.

"This tiger is a real miracle!" Tosha thought. "What a mighty beast, and so much affection and kindness in it!"

"And the yarn? What a brave fellow! Just soft wool – up against a tiger! And it was so brave! A true friend and protector! And you know what, I'll take the Tiger with me! You won't such a friendly tiger like this anywhere else!"

Having played enough, Tosha, the yarn and Purr continued their way along the coast together with their large, stripey friend. The sky brightened in the distance; the clouds began to break up. Sunset's golden rays shone down on the yarn, caressing it soft with the warmth of the sun, tenderly stroking the glistening threads. That moment, the yarn just wanted to be with the sun, and throw itself into the sun's arms. It closed his eyes and leaned forward, and let itself roll down the beach into the sea. A wave picked him up and pulled him down to the sea bed. The yarn felt as helpless caught in this weird whirlpool of events. He was no longer a yarn, but a thin rope, stretched out by the sea wave. He pulled and began to squirm like a snake. But it took a long time before he could figure out how to move. Suddenly he was enveloped by light coming from the depths.

He turned and saw the sun looking back at him.

"Hi little baby!" said the sun.

"Hello," the rope said politely, and just a little nervous. "Who are you?"

"I am Sun," the sun answered.

The rope was at a loss for words and worried about his situation.

"Oh, Sun, I'm so glad to hear from you! I thought about you all the time. You know I'm a lot like you..."

Before the thread finished, the sun began to wind the thread.

"You're not that much like me," the sun replied.

Soon the thread again turned into a ball.

"Now you look more like a little sun."

"Purr says that I look a lot like you!" said the ball

"Oh, sweet and curious ball, you are still so young! Don't you worry at all yet about who you should become in this life – just live, and play and do whatever you like." Sun replied. "Look. Here is my golden ray! It is the prettiest ray that I have! I'll give it to you! When you're in a tough spot, the ray will tell you what to do. With this ray, I'll always be by your side!"

And so the sun wove a golden ray into the woollen yarn. The yarn felt warm, and glowed all through. But then it felt the tug of the waves, and straightened into a rope again. But in a moment it became so dark, the yarn could only see an open mouth gaping in front of him. The sun vanished. The rope shut its eyes, and when it opened them again wondered: "Was that a dream? Or a nightmare?" But as soon as the rope thought of the sun, it at once felt warm and cost inside. All of a sudden, it began to glow like a light bulb, and saw that he was inside some kind of fish.

Big, big fish, let go of me!

I'm not a worm at all,

I'm a just little yarn ball, see!

And I'm really very small!

At the same moment, the rope felt a yank at its far end and felt someone pulling it to the shore. Soon it was in Tosha's arms on the beach, and she curled the little rope up into a proper ball of yarn again. The yarn looked around and saw that a large sardine that had swallowed a fishing rod's bait. The curious fish was unhooked and released back into the sea. "The fish thought I was a little worm?" The yarn concluded. "No wonder it swallowed me."

The waves in the sea are blue, blue, blue

And silver fish swim down below

But when the little yarn jumped in there too,

It got awfully wet, don't you know?

But Tosha's hands are so safe and warm

That the little yarn is much drier

All it needs now is just a little calm,

And a cosy night by the fire.

For a whlle Tosha, Purr, the yarn and the tiger lay on the shore. The first stars began to appear in the sky. The yarn thought of the crocodile, the strange sardine and the sun. It looked up and saw one star burst and fall like a spark. Purr said that when a star falls, a new soul is born on earth. It was the yarn's star, its soul, its golden ray. Soon the yarn dozed off, and didn't remember how Tosha brought it home, lit the fire and took out her knitting needles. After all the adventures, she realized who the yarn could be. She said to herself: "Since you are such a curious little fidget, I know just who you look like!" She quickly began to run the yarn through her hands and her knitting needles flashed back and forth, like a beautiful machine. An hour later, a woolly tail appeared, then a woolly body, two woolly paws and a cute woolly face. Tosha took a needle and sewed on a pair of silver buttons for the eyes and a brown nose.

"I will call you Sun!" Said Tosha, finishing her work. "Because you are very kind, warm and sweet!" Tosha lay Sun on the bed next to her, closed her eyes and fell asleep. The next morning, the one who used to be a ball of yarn woke up. It took three steps forward and fell off the bed onto the floor. Steady itself, it stood up and then began swaying and wobbling this way and that over the carpet in a very odd way. It couldn't understand what was happening. Rolling used to be so easy! It looked down and saw round, woolly paws. It lifted the right paw, sniffed it to make sure it didn't bite, then lifted the left paw and dropped it again.

"Rrrrr," he blurted out in annoyance.

Finally, he pulled himself right up.

"Am I standing on paws? How strange, I've never had legs in my life!"

As it was thinking about this weird turn of events, it immediately felt a huge butterfly that sat on the top of his head and spread its wings.

"Those are my ears!"

Immediately, he felt weak jolts and swaying behind him.

"My tail?"

From surprise, a loud "woof" escaped from him, and then another "woof" and another...

"Hello, my friend! Hello, my Sun! Hello, my puppy!" Tosha said in a sleepy voice.

The puppy wagged its tail even more and jumped on the floor.

Tosha took the puppy in her arms and hugged it tightly to her chest. And Sun licked her nose with its woolly puppy tongue. Sun struggled, trying to free itself from Tosha's tight embrace. So Tosha put the little woolly puppy on the floor and with paws flailing wildly it lolloped out of the room, almost knocking Purr over on his way, and raced out into the yard.

"What? He did he escape again?" Thought Tosha.

"Time for another adventure!" The cat meowed unperturbed.

THE END

ABOUT AUTHOR

Mihail Kunitsky Born in Zhodin, Belarus, on July 5th, 1986. He graduated from the Belarusian State University of Informatics and Radioelectronics. He currently collaborates with the publishing house "Azbukvarik". He was a finalist of the "Poet of the Year 2016, 2017, 2019 and 2020" award in the "Children's Literature" nomination. He was the winner of the 2007 International Youth Literary Competition named after the Schnittke Brothers in the nomination "For the style and culture of writing". At the 2017 "National Literary Prize Golden Pen of Rus'" competition he received the title of "Silver Pen of Rus'" in the "children's nomination". He took second place in the "Open Eurasia 2018" competition. He was the winner of the "Poet of the Year" award in 2019. He is a member of the union "TO DAR" (Creative Association of Children's Authors of Russia) and part of the Eurasian Creative Guild. He had published a book of children's poems in Moscow titled "Where Dreams Come From" in 2018. Then two more books after that titled "The World is So Unique," published in Moscow and "Journey on Four Legs," published in London, 2021.

Maria Shevel Prize was established for the fourth time in the history of the festival. The award is given to one contestant in the category of "Literary Work" for a work written in any language, in any genre, but which is dedicated to children's topics.

Maria Ivanovna Shevel – was an Uzbek architect who was born on May 1st, 1943 in the Sumy Region, Ukraine. After graduating from an education institute, she was sent to Central Asia, where she took part in the construction of the Toktogul hydroelectric power station in Kyrgyzstan. Since 1965, she worked under the personal guidance of Sharaf Rashidov on the development of the "Hungry Steppe" and the architectural appearance of the city of Jizzakh, Uzbekistan. She sincerely fell in love with her new homeland Uzbekistan and raised 5 children there. She was a winner of a number of state awards: Hero of Labor, Labor Veteran, Motherhood Medal and many others.

Printed in United Kingdom
Hertfordshire Press Ltd © 2022
e-mail: publisher@hertfordshirepress.com
www.hertfordshirepress.com

THE YARN NAMED SUN

MIKHAIL KUNITSKIY

English

illustrator: Albina Petrova
editor: John Farndon
translated from Russian: Timur Akhmedjanov
typeset: Alexandra Rey

British Library Catalogue in Publication Data
A catalogue record for this book is available from the British Library
Library of Congress in Publication Data
A catalogue record for this book has been requested

ISBN: 978-1-913356-60-6